P9-CFA-643

FRANCES WARD WELLER   ROBERT J. BLAKE

THE ANGEL OF

PHILOMEL BOOKS

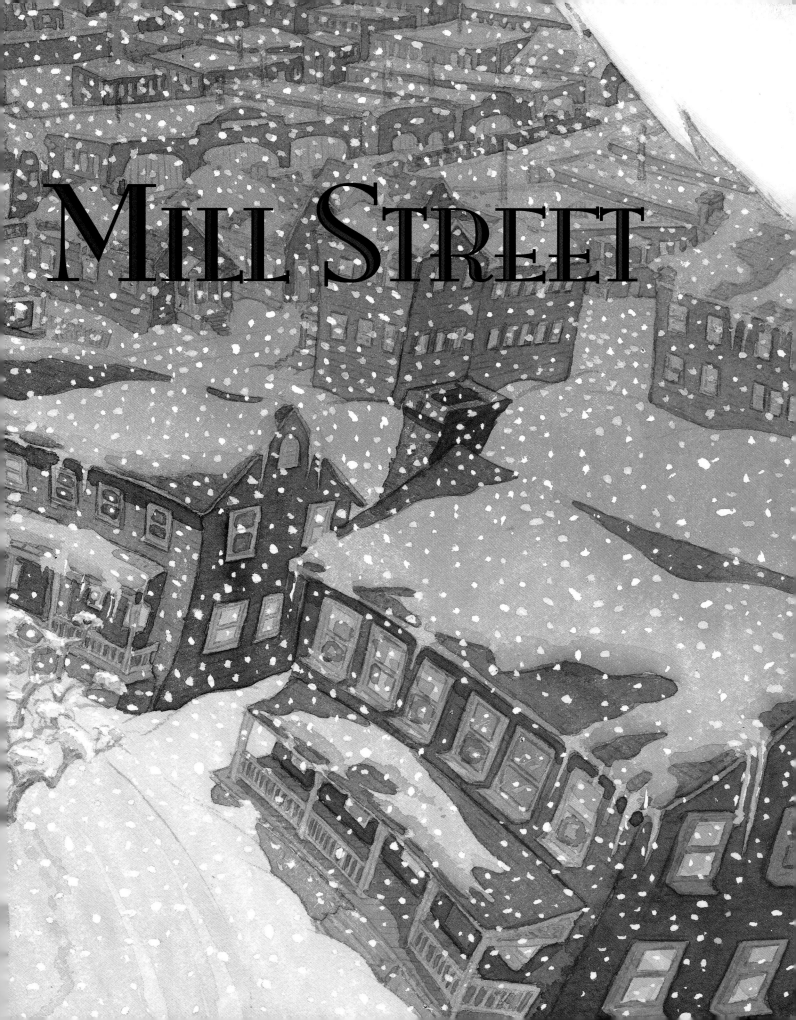

Mill Street

*O*ne *Christmas Eve* some hundred years ago, little Frances Rosalie Murphy waited. She waited for Saint Nicholas. She waited for the Christ child. But most urgently, she waited for her uncle, Ambrose Moriarty. Snow fell like curtains drawing 'round the house, and he had promised to be home for supper.

Especially this night she needed Uncle Ambrose. Christmas could never start without him — despite the fat fir tree with cranberry and popcorn garlands; despite the Christmas smells brought forth by Ma in flurries of cinnamon and flour; despite Pa's bass-bell reading of Saint Luke's gospel.

For it was Ambrose, with his fiddle and sweet, soaring voice — it was Uncle Ambrose who made Christmas sing. He'd sing Luke's story in a lullaby: "... angels did appear, which put the shepherds in great fear."

"But were there really angels?" Frances would ask, part of their Christmas ritual.

Uncle Ambrose would manage to shrug and nod at the same time, and carol on: "'Arise and go,' the angel said, 'to Bethlehem; be not afraid; for there you'll find, this happy morn, a princely Babe, sweet Jesus, born!'"

"'Arise and go,'" whispered Frances as she swept the kitchen floor. "'Be not afraid'—but oh, be careful!" For it was snowing hard, and just a bit of snow was a dangerous thing for Ambrose Moriarty.

Truth was that Uncle Ambrose needed looking after. As a lad in far-off County Kerry, he had romped in a lumberyard against all good advice, and there he fell and broke his leg. The leg was never set properly. So the boy who had nimbly leaped log mountains grew up crippled, with a limp and pain that never left him quite alone.

With his quick wit and minstrel's voice, Ambrose was always welcome where folks gathered to sing their sad, fierce songs of Ireland. He sang at weddings, and at dances played his fiddle. And when he roamed the town late and laughing, as he did this Christmas Eve, Frances Rosalie sorely missed him.

Oh, they'd a lot to be thankful for this Christmas Eve day, Ma reminded her. For stockings that would not be empty, for the turkey that waited in the pantry, for this lace-curtain home on the clean outskirts of the sooty mill town. Blessed are the meek, Ma always said.

True enough, thought Frances Rosalie. But Ma was forever busy. And Pa, gone by sunup, came home bone-tired from work in the boot factory. So when Frances needed a song, a story, or a chuckle, it was Uncle Ambrose she went after.

Through the lace curtains in the parlor, Frances spied snowflakes still falling steadily. There'd be fine sledding on Glover's Hill if the sled she longed for was under the tree tomorrow. And even the grim brick woolen factory at the other end of Mill Street would look clean tonight, for the snow worked magic, made everything smell fresh and new. It fell like a blessing on her world, a fitting welcome for the Christ child. But she wanted to share it with Uncle Ambrose.

Why had he not stamped in long since, to lurch around the kitchen humming carols and raiding Ma's bowl of turkey stuffing?

When Ma heard it was still snowing, the fine lines between her brows began to deepen. Her gaze turned often to the clock. She fretted when Pa stomped in, weary, demanding supper and sleep before the long walk to Midnight Mass. With too much snow, they might not get to church. With too much snow, the cousins might miss tomorrow's dinner.

As supper of creamed codfish and boiled potatoes came and went, the snow piled higher and the wind howled louder. Worse, Frances knew, was the worry left unspoken: With too much snow, Ambrose might not get home at all.

If Ambrose fell with no one there to help him to his feet, the snow could be a freezing, deadly blanket.

*N*o, *he might not* make it home at all. But knowing Ambrose, he was bound to try. The way was long and dark and biting, bitter cold—two miles and more, across the bridge where wind swept down the river, past the boot mill, past the green watched over by the Yankees' tall white houses on the hill. Past looming shadows of the woolen mill. Last, down the long black road with house lights scattered like first stars of evening.

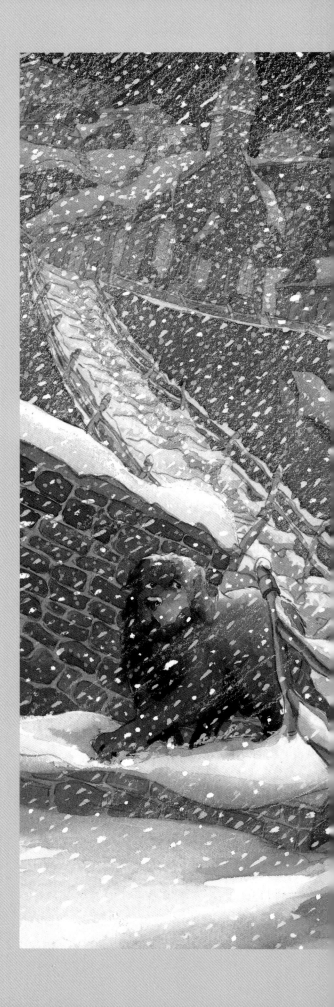

Frances walked the whole way in her mind as Ma grew furious. "How he could do this! I can hear him now, 'Just one more chorus to speed me home!' And himself a grown-up person, and this Christmas Eve!"

Frances helped her older sisters wash the dishes. They set the stuffing in the pantry. They tucked the little brothers into bed. The wind seemed now to fling itself against the house. Frances ran again to the parlor window. The storm was weaving white veils on the panes, but where light fell from the house she could see snow drifting along the picket fence. Landmarks were disappearing. "Oh, God, please take care of Uncle Ambrose," she breathed against the icy glass.

In the kitchen rocker by the wood-stove, Ma sat with her eyes closed, fingering her rosary. The girls bent over knitting, putting the last stitches in sweaters for the younger children, but nervous fingers fumbled. Ma made the sign of the cross and opened her eyes.

"It's a judgment on me," she cried. "Fussin' over pies and Christmas Eve delights, and him flound'rin' in a drift, or freezin' in a gutter! I'm goin' to wake Pa!

"No human soul would be out to shepherd the likes of Ambrose on such a night, and it Christmas Eve!"

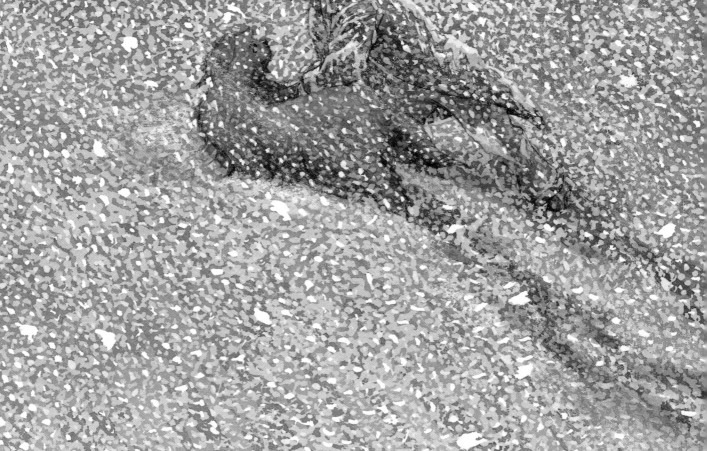

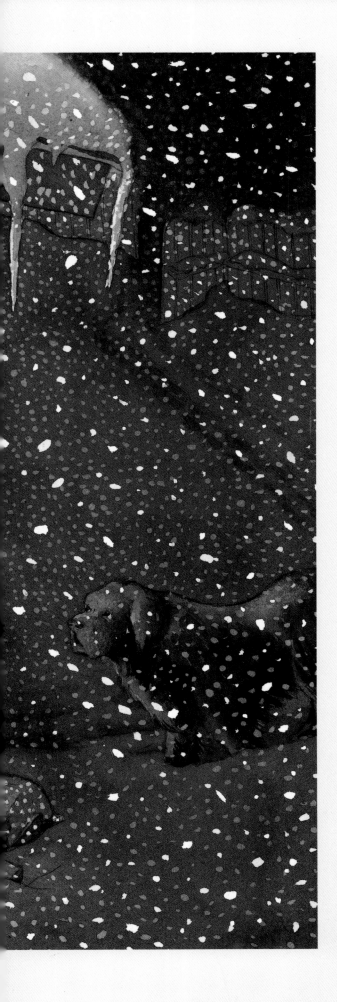

*A*nd *then below* the howling of the wind came a shuffling sound on the porch. Jo and Lalie leaped to their feet, and a chair crashed on the hearth. Ma spun back into the room with eyes alight, and Frances rushed to open the door.

A gust of wind showered starry crystals across the kitchen, and the rush of cold was like a fist driving into the cozy room.

There leaning against the porch upright was himself, Uncle Ambrose Moriarty.

He'd been in more than one snowdrift, by the look of him, and his bad leg dragged at a weary angle, but he was home.

Frances leaped into the knee-deep snow on the porch to hug her uncle, but stopped with a gasp as something moved behind him.

In the shadows just beyond the lamplight, a massive hairy shape seemed to take form from the wind and snow itself. A great black dog with bottomless dark eyes lifted one front paw to the porch, and then the other.

For a long moment the creature stared into the lamplight. He turned his heavy head to the hand Ambrose lifted to him and gave it a long lick. Then, with a single motion, he leaped and turned and melted back into the storm.

"Oh, please come back!" Frances called after him. But he was gone.

"What was that?" Lalie cried.

"Biggest dog I ever saw," muttered Ambrose. "Or else my guardian angel."

Ambrose was shaking, but his grin was steady as he held Frances away a bit so he could look her in the eye. He nodded with no shrug at all. "If there were angels above that hill in Bethlehem," he said, "why not an angel here on Mill Street?"

Well, they put Ambrose to bed with hot tea, and hot bricks wrapped in cloth, and they gave up hope of getting to Midnight Mass in such a storm. Christmas morning dawned on a sled beneath the tree for Frances, and Uncle Ambrose tuning up his fiddle.

But what Frances would treasure most about that Christmas was the memory of Uncle Ambrose and the big black dog. For questions asked all 'round the town revealed that no such dog was ever known, before or after.

Author's Note

All her long life, Frances Rosalie would tell that story, whenever a child or grandchild or great-grandchild asked if she believed in angels.

"Maybe it matters less if you believe in them, than if they believe in you," said my grandmother Frances Rosalie. "The way that one believed in Uncle Ambrose Moriarty."

This is for Hannah and Colleen,
Frances Rosalie's great-great-granddaughters.

—F. W.

To my own Guardian Angel.

—R. B.

PATRICIA LEE GAUCH, EDITOR

Text copyright © 1998 by Frances Ward Weller. Illustrations copyright © 1998 by Robert J. Blake. All rights reserved. This book, or parts thereof, may not be reproduced in any form without permission in writing from the publisher, Philomel Books, a division of The Putnam & Grosset Group, 200 Madison Avenue, New York, NY 10016. Philomel Books, Reg. U.S. Pat. & Tm. Off. Published simultaneously in Canada. Printed in Hong Kong by South China Printing Co. (1988) Ltd. Book design by Cecilia Yung and Donna Mark. The text is set in Columbus.

Library of Congress Cataloging-in-Publication Data Weller, Frances Ward. Angel of Mill street/Frances Ward Weller; illustrated by Robert J. Blake p. cm. Summary: On a snowy Christmas eve in the late 1800s, Frances and her family wait and worry when beloved Uncle Ambrose, who has a crippled leg, does not come home as expected. [1. Uncles—Fiction. 2. Christmas—Fiction. 3. Family life—Fiction. 4. Physically handicapped—Fiction. 5. Ireland—Fiction.] I. Blake, Robert J., ill. II. Title. PZ7.W454An 1998 [Fic]—DC21 97-21483 CIP AC ISBN 0-399-23133-1
3 5 7 9 10 8 6 4 2